KT-162-051

PUFFIN BOOKS

WAR GAME

Michael Foreman was born in Suffolk. He studied at
Lowestoft Art School and then at the Royal College of
Art, where he graduated with first class honours. He
has worked on magazines, as an illustrator and art
director, and in film animation. For twenty years he
has also been the art editor of the literary magazine
Ambit. He is still best known, however, for his work
as an author and illustrator of children's books and
has been the winner of the Kurt Maschler Award, the
Kate Greenaway Medal, the Children's Book Award
and twice winner of the Francis Williams Illustration
Award. *War Boy* recently won Michael Foreman the
Kate Greenaway Medal for the second time.

Also by Michael Foreman

WAR BOY: A COUNTRY CHILDHOOD
AFTER THE WAR WAS OVER

Michael Foreman

WAR GAME

PUFFIN BOOKS

PUFFIN BOOKS

Published by the Penguin Group
Penguin Books Ltd, 27 Wrights Lane, London W8 5TZ, England
Penguin Books USA Inc., 375 Hudson Street, New York, New York 10014, USA
Penguin Books Australia Ltd, Ringwood, Victoria, Australia
Penguin Books Canada Ltd, 10 Alcorn Avenue, Toronto, Ontario, Canada M4V 3B2
Penguin Books (NZ) Ltd, 182–190 Wairau Road, Auckland 10, New Zealand

Penguin Books Ltd, Registered Offices: Harmondsworth, Middlesex, England

First published by Pavilion Books Limited 1989
Published in Puffin Books 1995
7 9 10 8

THE KICK-OFF

Goal! Will saw the ball hit the back of the net. In his imagination he had just scored for England, and he heard the roar of a huge crowd. But he knew that around the pitch there was no crowd, just a low hedge and the familiar flat fields of the Suffolk countryside.

A group of small boys jumped around behind the goal and a few old men sitting under the elms clapped. The church clock struck five. The game was over.

'Most of them are joining the army,' said Freddie, the goalkeeper. 'We should, really.'

'I'd like to,' said Billy, eyes shining with excitement.

'No, you're too young. If you went, I'd have to go to look after you,' laughed his big brother Lacey.

'It *would* be an adventure though,' said Will. 'And they say it'll be over by Christmas. Be a pity to miss it.'

And so they talked as they wandered back along the dusty lane into the village.

The summer of 1914 had been one of the hottest ever, and while Will and his friends had worked long and hard in the harvest fields, far away in a place called Sarajevo an archduke had been killed. The German emperor, Kaiser Bill, was using the confusion as an excuse to start a war and seize territory from his neighbouring countries.

'So once again the British Army has to go overseas and sort things out,' said the old men of the village over their pints of beer.

Many of the old soldiers of the village had already been recalled to the army and were on their way to the battlefields of France and Belgium. There was a lot of pressure on the young men to follow them. The British Army needed many thousands of men to stop the Germans advancing across Europe. Recruitment posters were everywhere, and the newspapers called on every man to do his duty 'for King and Country'.

THE VETERAN'S FAREWELL.

"Good Bye, my lad,
I only wish I were young enough
to go with you!"

ENLIST NOW!

The day after the football match was a Sunday, and the vicar boomed out the same message from his pulpit. The local squire, in the front pew, wore all the medals he could get his hands on, and his son wore a brand-new, tailor-made officer's uniform. After the service, Will, Freddie, Billy and Lacey sat by the signpost under the oak and the elm at the corner of the green. Here they had sat almost every day of their lives, after church, after school and after work.

'I think we should join,' said Freddie. 'None of us has ever been outside the county. It's time we saw something of the world.'

'Yes! An adventure – and home by Christmas,' said Billy.

Will wasn't so sure. After all, he thought, a lot of people can get killed in a war. But they agreed that next day after work, they would go into town and see what was happening at the Town Hall, the local army recruiting office.

THE ADVENTURE

They had never seen such a crowd. There was a
great feeling of excitement and even of fun as the
flags waved and the band played. Every time a lad
went to join up, the crowd gave him a hearty cheer.

Before anyone could stop him, Billy was up the
steps and the crowd was cheering him. Then Freddie
followed. Lacey had to go to look after Billy. Will

knew he couldn't let his friends go off to war without him, so to wild cheers all four joined the army. They were given railway warrants and told to report to barracks in four days' time.

They had a lot of explaining to do when they got home that evening.

4 Questions to the Women of England

1. YOU have read what the Germans have done in Belgium. Have you thought what they would do if they invaded England?

2. Do you realise that the Safety of your Home and Children depends on our getting more men _now_?

3. Do you realise that the one word "Go" from _you_ may send another man to fight for our King and Country?

4. When the War is over and your husband or your son is asked, "What did you do in the great War?"—is he to hang his head because _you_ would not let him go?

... of England do ... Send your men t... ur glorious Arm...

...ave the K...

4 Questions to Clerks and Shop Assistants.

1. If you are between 19 and 38 years of age, are you really satisfied with what you are doing to-day?

2. Do you feel happy as you walk along the streets and see brave men in khaki who are going to _fight_ for the Empire while you stay at home in comfort?

3. Do you _realise_ that our gallant ... g everything on ... ave you, your ... r womenfolk?

... employer _to-day_ ... to _enlist_?

... e position open ... m that you are ... or the Empire, ... thing by you— ... pers are helping

...NOW AND

...TO-DAY.

...THE KING.

Is One Dear to You Fighting in the Great War?

If so you are entitled to **WEAR THIS BADGE.**

It is worn by women who have a relative or sweetheart serving.

Send 1/-

and the name of the one serving to: The Woman's Branch, National Service, 63, Temple Chambers, London, E.C.

The Pendant of Service and Sacrifice.

"We Must All Fall In," the National Service Marching Song, can be obtained (post free 7d.) from the same address.

5 Questions to patriotic Shopkeepers

1. HAVE you any fit men between 19 and 38 years of age serving behind your counter who at this moment ought to be serving their country?

2. Will you call your male employees together and explain to them that in order to end the War quickly we must have more men?

3. Will you tell them what you are prepared to do for them whilst they are fighting for the Empire?

4. Have you realised that we cannot have "business as usual" whilst the War continues?

THE ARMY WANTS MORE MEN TO-DAY

5. Could not Women or older men fill their places till the War is over?

YOUR COUNTRY WILL APPRECIATE THE HELP YOU GIVE.

God Save the King.

Are **YOU** in this?

Being country boys, they were all good shots, and they were signed into the King's Royal Rifles. It sounded very grand. But so great was the rush to join that the army was overwhelmed with recruits and didn't have enough uniforms for them all. Will and the other lads were disappointed and felt foolish learning the basic training and drills wearing their ordinary clothes. They slept in bell tents in a huge field, about a dozen men to a tent. The food was poor and the days were long and exhausting.

However, after a few weeks they were all kitted out and the 'adventure' had really started. They boarded a P&O ship in Southampton and prepared to set sail at six o'clock in a great convoy.

The whole of Southampton turned out to see
them off. Thousands of sailors cheered and waved
their caps from destroyers in Southampton
Water.

As the coast of England faded behind them, Will, like the countless young men crowded around him, felt strangely alone with his thoughts of home and of what lay over the horizon.

'Come on, lads. Let's have a song,' called Freddie. They sang as they sailed and felt better.

TO THE FRONT

When they reached France they were packed
into trains, which stopped and started and
crawled all day along the overcrowded
tracks.

The country didn't look so different. People worked the fields just as the lads had done back home. Some of the workers unbent their backs and waved as the trains went by.

The soldiers finally arrived at a small station
that had grown into a vast supply depot. Trains
and trucks were being shunted and unloaded.

Mountains of stores, horse lines and mule lines
were everywhere, and there was a babel of
shouted commands.

Then at last they were off the trains and marching.
Will felt good to be out in the fresh air and swinging
along with his mates. Marching through villages and
towns, the troops were cheered all the way. Flowers,

Then things began to change. The roads became crowded with people moving back from the Front. The whole population seemed to be on the move. Families carried their children and pushed prams loaded with whatever they could salvage from their lives. No more cheering crowds. These people had seen war. Their homes had been blown to bits, their farms criss-crossed by armies, trenches, wire, and pock-marked by a million artillery shells. Will could hear the almost continuous sound of shellfire in the distance.

They passed wagons full of wounded soldiers on their way back to England, and long lines of exhausted ragged troops sitting in the mud, rain and gathering darkness before being ordered back into the action.

At last the marching came to an end, and Will,
Freddie, Lacey and Billy and the rest of the brigade
were ordered on to a fleet of London General
omnibuses that were to rush them up to the Front to
fill a gap in the 'Line'. They drove through the ruins
of a devastated town. The lads had never been to
London, yet here they were riding on a London

bus in the middle of France. The conductor's bell
was still working, and one of the men kept ringing
it and shouting 'Next stop Piccadilly Circus!' The
glassless windows were covered with boards, but
there were plenty of holes to peep through. Will's
first reaction was: 'Doesn't it look pretty? Just like
fireworks.'

Lavatories, or latrines, were dug at the end of short trenches, mostly to the rear of the main trench. Occasionally they were dug a little way forward into No Man's Land to discourage anyone from lingering too long.

Then they were in the trenches. Not the Front trench, but the reserve. In single file they moved forward along a winding communication trench to the support trench. Here they waited with the sound of battle exploding all around them.

There was a lull.

'All right, lads. It's our turn,' said their sergeant, and in single file and pouring rain they squelched along another communication trench to the Front.

The trenches of the Western Front crossed Belgium and France for a distance of 460 miles. The Front trench was about three feet wide at the bottom and seven feet high. To enable the soldiers to fire over or through the parapet, a fire-step was built two feet high into the forward side of the trench. It was on this that the sentries stood to keep watch.

There was still no shooting on this section of the Line as Will and his mates crouched on the fire-step to allow wounded and exhausted soldiers to pass by on their way to the rear.

Dogs were sometimes used as sentries in some sections, particularly by the French. Some dogs also searched for wounded men and others were messenger dogs.

NO MAN'S LAND

Will and Freddie were the first to be posted as
sentries on their little section, and, cautiously, they
stood up on the fire-step. They peered over the
parapet into No Man's Land. They could just see their

own first line of wire and random humps and bumps in an otherwise flat landscape that seeped rapidly into darkness. A landscape as flat as the fields of home.

Then a flare arced and spiralled slowly from the sky. Will and Freddie could see that the humps and bumps were men. Dead men. Some of them, who had cut their trousers into shorts during the hot weather, looked like fallen schoolboys.

Before the flare faded, Will and Freddie saw more
lines of wire and, beyond No Man's Land, the front
line of German trenches.

'Less than a goal-kick away,' whispered
Freddie.

The newcomers quickly learned the routine of trench life. An hour before dawn every morning they received the order to 'Stand To'. Half asleep and frozen, the men climbed on to the fire-step, rifles clutched with numb fingers and bayonets fixed.

The half light of dawn and dusk was when an attack was most expected, and both sides had their trenches fully manned at those times. Sometimes nothing happened. Often there was a furious exchange of rifle and machine-gun fire to discourage any attack through the gloom. This was known as 'morning hate'.

After an hour or so the order was given to 'Stand Down'. Only the sentries remained on the fire-step and the rest of the men enjoyed what breakfast they could get among the rats, blood-red slugs and horned beetles that infested the trenches.

Each company going to the Front Line took food for three days, usually bully beef, tins of jam and bone-hard biscuit. Army biscuit had to be smashed with a shovel or bayonet. The pieces were then soaked in water for a couple of days and were sometimes added to soup.

Dugouts were dug into the sides of trenches and roofed with timber or corrugated iron and covered with a minimum of 9 inches of earth and sandbags.

Sometimes the rats would suddenly disappear. Old soldiers thought this to be a sure sign of imminent heavy shelling.

As the weather grew worse, the two huge armies became bogged down in virtually fixed positions. In some places they were only thirty yards apart, so close that the heavy guns, firing from behind the reserve lines, often killed their own men when shells fell short of their target.

The mud became deeper and deeper as thousands of men, mules, horses and heavy wagons and guns churned it up.

*The Germans sometimes
used a flare suspended
from a small parachute.
This blazed brightly for
up to a minute, and might
be followed by a second
and a third flare.*

Now and then the soldiers were ordered to
attack across No Man's Land, even though many
lives were always lost and little or nothing was
achieved. Small raiding parties ventured out at
night to cause as much damage as they could,
and, if possible, to return with a prisoner or two who
could provide some useful information. Other small

teams were sent to repair or lay new wire. The
covering darkness could be suddenly illuminated
at any time by flares. A pistol flare remained bright
for about fifteen seconds. This seemed an eternity
to men lying motionless in No Man's Land await-
ing the rattle of machine-gun fire or a sniper's
bullet.

"TUBS FOR TOMMIES."

£10 WILL PROVIDE A UNIT OF 4 BATHS.
WITH STOVE, BOILER, TOWELS, SOAP, SCRUBBERS
AND ALL EQUIPMENT.

FROM
THE EMERGENCY VOLUNTARY AID COMMITTEE
OF THE EMPRESS CLUB
DOVER STREET W.

SOAP

APPLY TO THE SECRETARY, BRANCH OFFICE 56, QUEEN VICTORIA ST. E.C.

*Steel helmets were devised in 1915. In short supply,
they were passed from one man to another as the
soldiers left the firing line. The Battle of the Somme
in 1916 was the first time that all the British soldiers
had their own helmets.*

The communication trenches were particularly busy at night. Dead and wounded were carried to the rear, and food and munitions were brought to the Front. When possible the dead were recovered from No Man's Land. Like clearing the table after dinner, ready for the generals' next game of soldiers, Will thought.

Will often thought of his family sleeping peacefully just a hundred miles away, and of his own bed, dry and warm under the thatched eaves of home. Even his old dog guarding the yard and the pigs in the byre lived in more comfort than Will and the British Army.

And still it rained.

The water table of this flat land was often less than three feet below the surface. Every shell hole filled with water. The trenches were awash with mud. Here and there men hollowed out little caves or 'scrapes' in the sides of the trenches to give them some protection from the rain, but they had little protection from the high-explosive shells, which could rain down at any moment.

The enemy trenches were so close that whenever the fighting died down, each army could hear the other's voices and could sometimes even smell their breakfast. They all knew that they were sharing the same terrible conditions.

Singing in the trenches was common in 1914, and songs from one front line floated to the other on the quiet evening air. Occasionally during a quiet period a British Tommy would put a tin can on a stick and hold it above the parapet to give the Germans some shooting practice. The Germans would do likewise with tin cans or bottles, and a shooting match would develop accompanied by cheers and boos.

The primitive war-planes of 1914 were not armed at first and flew on spy missions, spotting enemy gun positions, supply depots and troop movements.

Pilot and observer were usually armed with revolver and rifle respectively. Some carried grenades, which they tried to drop on the trenches.

Sometimes the soldiers watched rival aircraft confront each other in mid-air duels over the trenches.

Will, Freddie, Lacey and Billy stayed together as much as possible and lived like bedraggled moles in a world of mud, attack and counter-attack.

The weather, still wet, grew steadily colder. Then, one night, as the lads returned to the Front after a few days' rest, the rain stopped and it grew bitterly cold.

That night they were relieving a Scottish regiment, and as the Scots left the Line, the Germans shouted Christmas wishes to them.

Then tiny lights appeared in the German trenches.
As far as the eye could see, Christmas trees were
flickering along the parapet of the German lines.

It was Christmas Eve.

A single German voice began to sing 'Silent Night'.
It was joined by many others.

The British replied with 'The First Noel' to applause from the Germans. And so it went on, turn and turn about. Then both front lines sang 'O Come All Ye Faithful'.

It was a beautiful moonlit night. Occasionally a star shell hung like a Star of Bethlehem.

At dawn, when the British were all 'Stood To'
on the fire-step, they saw a world white with frost.
The few shattered trees that remained were white.
Lines of wire glinted like tinsel. The humps of
dead in No Man's Land were like toppled
snowmen.

 After the singing of the night, the Christmas

dawn was strangely quiet. The clock of death had stopped ticking.

Then a German climbed from his trench and planted a Christmas tree in No Man's Land. Freddie, being a goalkeeper and therefore a bit daft, walked out and shook hands with him. Both sides applauded.

A small group of men from each side,
unarmed, joined them. They all shook hands.
One of the Germans spoke good English

and said he hoped the war would end soon because
he wanted to return to his job as a taxi driver
in Birmingham.

It was agreed that they should take the opportunity
to bury the dead. The bodies were mixed up together.

They were sorted out, and a joint burial service was
held on the 'halfway line'.

With our best wishes for
Christmas 1914
May God protect you and
bring you home safe
Mary R   George R.I.

Both sides then returned to their trenches for breakfast. Will and the lads were cheered by the wonderful smell of bacon, and they had a hot breakfast for a change.

One by one, birds began to arrive from all sides. The soldiers hardly ever saw a bird normally, but Will counted at least fifty sparrows hopping around their trench.

Christmas presents for the men consisted of a packet of chocolate, Oxo cubes, a khaki handkerchief, peppermints, camp cocoa, writing paper and a pencil. After breakfast a pair of horses and a wagon arrived with Princess Mary's Christmas gifts – a pipe and tobacco and a Christmas card from the King and Queen.

There were no planes overhead, no observation balloons, no bombs, no rifle fire, no snipers, just an occasional skylark. The early mist lifted to reveal a clear blue sky. The Germans were strolling about on their parapet once more, and waved to the British to join them. Soon there was quite a crowd in No Man's Land. Both sides exchanged small gifts. One German had been a barber in Holborn in London. A chair was placed on the 'halfway line', and he gave haircuts to several of the British soldiers.

Then, from somewhere, a football bounced across the frozen mud. Will was on it in a flash. He trapped the ball with his left foot, flipped it up with his right, and headed it towards Freddie.

Freddie made a spectacular dive, caught the ball in both hands and threw it to a group of Germans.

Immediately a vast, fast and furious football match was under way. Goals were marked by caps. Freddie, of course, was in one goal and a huge German in the other.

Apart from that, it was wonderfully disorganized,
part football, part ice-skating, with unknown
numbers on each team. No referee,
no account of the score.

It was just terrific to be no longer an army of moles, but up and running on top of the ground that had threatened to entomb them for so long. And this time Will really could hear a big crowd – and he *was* playing for England!

He was playing in his usual centre forward position with Lacey to his left and little Billy on the wing. The game surged back and forth across No Man's Land. The goalposts grew larger as greatcoats and tunics were discarded as the players warmed to the sport. Khaki and grey mixed together. Steam rose from their backs, and their faces were wreathed in smiles and clouds of breath in the clear frosty air.

Some of the British officers took a dim view of such sport, and when the game came to its exhausted end, the men were encouraged back to their trenches for a carol service and supper. The haunting sound of men singing drifted back and forth across No Man's Land in the still night air.

'Good night, Tommies. See you tomorrow.'

'Good night, Fritz. We'll have another game.'

But Boxing Day passed without a game. The officers were alarmed at what had happened on Christmas Day. If such friendly relations continued, how could they get the men to fight again? How could the war continue?

The men were not allowed to leave the trenches. There were a few secret meetings here and there along the Front, and gifts and souvenirs were exchanged.

Two more days passed peacefully. Then a message was thrown over from the German side. A very important general was due to visit their section at 3.15 that afternoon and he would want to see some action. The Germans therefore would start firing at 3 p.m. and the Tommies should please keep their heads down.

At three o'clock a few warning shots were fired over the British trenches and then heavy fire lasted for an hour. The Tommies kept their heads down.

It was the Duke of Wellington who gave the nickna.
'Tommy' to the British soldiers. When asked in 1843 to think
of a name typical of the private soldier, the great duke
thought back over his long career to his first campaign in the
Low Countries. He remembered a group of wounded
men lying on the ground. One of them had a sabre slash in
his head, a bayonet wound in his chest, and a bullet through
his lungs. He begged not to be moved, but left to die in peace.
He must have seen Wellington's concern. 'It's all right, sir,' he
gasped. 'It's all in a day's work.'
'What's your name, soldier?' the Duke asked.
'Thomas Atkins, sir.'
They were his last words.

At dawn a few days later, the Germans mounted
a full-scale attack. The friendly Germans from
Saxony had been withdrawn and replaced by

fresh troops from Prussia. They were met by rapid and deadly fire from the British and were forced back.

The order was given to counter-attack, to try to take the German trenches before they could reorganize themselves. Will and the rest of the soldiers scrambled over the parapet.

Freddie still had the football! He drop-kicked it far
into the mist of No Man's Land.

'That'll give someone a surprise,' he said.

'Why are goalies always daft?' thought Will.

They were on the attack. Running in a line, Will in a centre forward position, Lacey to his left, young Billy on the wing.

From the corner of his eye Will saw Freddie dive full-length, then curl up as if clutching a ball in the best goalkeeping tradition.

'Daft as a brush,' Will thought.

Suddenly they all seemed to be tackled at once. The whole line went down. Earth and sky turned over, and Will found himself in a shell hole staring at the sky. Then everything went black.

Slowly the blackness cleared and Will could see the
hazy sky once more. Bits of him felt hot and other
bits felt very cold. He couldn't move his legs. He
heard a slight movement. There was someone else in
the shell hole.

Will dimly recognized the gleam of a fixed bayonet
and the outline of a German.

'*Wasser. Wasser*,' the German said.

It was about the only German word Will knew.
He fumbled for his water bottle and managed to push
it towards the German with the butt of his rifle.

The German drank deeply. He didn't have the
strength to return the bottle.

'*Kinder?*' he said. Will shook his head. The German
held up three fingers. Will tried to shake his head
again to show that he did not understand, but the
blackness returned.

Later he saw a pale ball of gold in the misty sky.
'There's a ball in Heaven,' he thought. 'Thank God.
We'll all have a game when this nightmare's over.'
At home when he had a bad dream he knew if he

opened his eyes, the bad dream would end. But here,
his eyes were already open.

Perhaps if he closed them, the nightmare would end.

He closed his eyes.

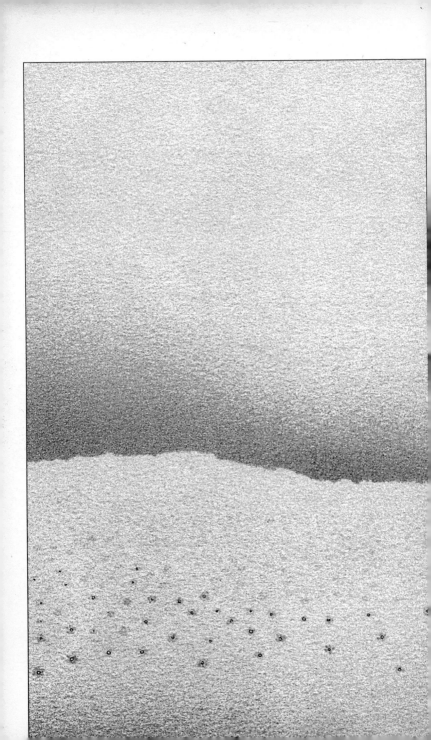